For Anna, who was accidentally born human

Petunia Goes Wild
Copyright © 2012 by Paul Schmid
All rights reserved. Manufactured in China.
No part of this book may be used or reproduced in any manner whatsoever without written permission except
in the case of brief quotations embodied in critical articles and reviews. For information address HarperCollins
Children's Books, a division of HarperCollins Publishers, 10 East 53rd Street, New York, NY 10022.
www.harpercollinschildrens.com

Library of Congress Cataloging-in-Publication Data
Schmid, Paul.
    Petunia goes wild / by Paul Schmid. — 1st ed.
        p.   cm.
    Summary: Petunia decides to stop being a human child and start living the life of a wild animal, much to her
parents' displeasure.
    ISBN 978-0-06-196334-6 (trade bdg.) — ISBN 978-0-06-196335-3 (lib. bdg.)
    [1. Behavior—Fiction.   2. Parent and child—Fiction.   3. Humorous stories.]   I. Title.
PZ7.S3492Ph   2012   2011001888
[E]—dc22   CIP
                                                                                                              AC

Typography by Dana Fritts   12 13 14 15 16   SCP   10 9 8 7 6 5 4 3 2 1   ❖   First Edition

paul schmid

Petunia
goes wild

HARPER
An Imprint of HarperCollinsPublishers

Monday morning Petunia, growling and snorting, ate her breakfast off the kitchen floor.

RARH!

Tuesday saw Petunia running around the front yard roaring at anyone who walked by.

On Wednesday Petunia, wearing no more than a smile, bathed in a mud puddle.

Thursday Petunia informed her parents
that she needed a cave to live in.

She was urged by her parents to
"Stop all this nonsense.

"You are *not* an animal," they added.

But Petunia felt that there had
been some mistake.

She really should have been
born an animal.
Being human was just too . . .

. . . clean.

Too careful.

Too clothed.

Too combed.

Too quiet.

Too . . . *hafta.*

Petunia made her parents a reasonable offer: "Can I be your pet instead?"

But her parents showed few signs
of being reasonable.

"No, you may *NOT!*

Where *did* **you get such an idea?** **Of** all the crazy things! That is **NOT** how nice little girls behave. **Rules** are there for a *reason*. What kind of parents would let their daughter run around on a **leash**? I can only *imagine* what the neighbors would say. *Most* parents we know have children who WANT to be children! You don't know how *lucky* you are to be a child. It's not that easy being an adult, I can tell you. . . .

Petunia needed to escape.

Soon she would be
wild and free!

Petunia got in.

Petunia sat waiting
to be delivered.

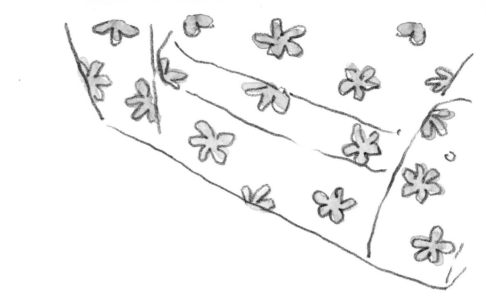

She could hear her mom
singing in the kitchen.

Tigers did not sing, thought Petunia.

Or tickle at bedtime, neither.

Petunia climbed out of the box
and quietly slid it into her room.

Whenever things got too human-ish,
Petunia decided, she'd have a
wild place of her own.

Then Petunia crept silently
back to the kitchen to listen
to her mom sing.